THE EMPEROR'S OLD CLOTHES

Kathryn Lasky

ILLUSTRATED BY David Catrow

Harcourt Brace & Company

San Diego   New York   London

Printed in Singapore

For Matthew Schnitzer —K. L.

For David, my son, man to man —D. C.

There once was a simple farmer named Henry. Henry lived on a small farm with some sheep, a cow, and a few chickens and goats. He wove cloth from his sheep's wool. He made omelettes from his chickens' eggs. He made butter and cheese from the cow's and goats' milk. Whatever he didn't use himself, he took to market to sell.

Henry always thanked his animals for what they gave him. I *am a blessed man,* he would think as he ate a cheese omelette or drank a glass of fresh milk. He loved his animals and his animals loved him.

One day, Henry was especially tired as he returned home from market. The marketplace had been noisier than usual that day because it was the emperor's birthday. Everyone had come to market to prepare for the holiday parties, and excitement about the birthday parade was in the air. The whole town was buzzing about the new finery the emperor would wear for the festivities. *Too much commotion!* Henry thought. *Too much hubbub!* He longed for the company of his animals and the peace of his farm.

Just before Henry turned onto the long road that ran past the palace, he heard a roar and a clatter. A carriage skidded around the curve and raced toward him. Henry jumped into a ditch just in time.

"Lunatics!" Henry shouted. "Nincom—" But before he could finish, something light and silky fluttered out of the carriage and into his face. Henry peeled off one piece, then another. He had never felt anything so smooth and fine between his callused fingers. He looked at the pieces carefully. They were long and narrow, and each had an odd footlike shape at the end.

"Well, I'll be a goat in a boat!" Henry murmured in awe. He had heard about silk stockings such as these. Kings and emperors wore them. They felt so smooth on his face—how would they feel on his feet? Dare he try them on? Henry looked around nervously, then crouched behind a squat bush, removed his heavy boots and thick socks, and wriggled his legs into the silk stockings.

"Chickie feathers!" he exclaimed with delight, for the only thing softer than those silk stockings was the fuzz of a newborn chick. He pulled on his boots and continued toward home.

Henry had not gone far when he spotted a strange shape in the middle of the road ahead. "A bird with a broken wing!" Henry cried. "Pig droppings on those maniacs in that speeding carriage—hitting a bird in flight!" He rushed closer, and realized that what he had seen was not a bird with a broken wing but a shoe. He picked it up and admired it, then looked around quickly. I *must try it on*, he thought.

His stockinged foot slipped right in. The fit was perfect. Walking was difficult, though, for the high-heeled shoe made one leg longer than the other. So it was most fortunate that Henry soon saw the shoe's mate. He took off his other heavy boot, slipped on the shoe, and walked proudly down the road. How grand he felt, and how much better the view was from his new height. *My animals back at the farm will hardly recognize me,* Henry thought. *I'll have to be careful not to step in any mud puddles or cow patties.*

The road continued uphill. When Henry reached the top, which was not easy in his elegant shoes, he saw a most peculiar fruit growing on the lowest branch of a tree. Immense and round, the fruit glittered in the sunlight.

"What gigantic peaches!" Henry cried, and his mouth began to water. He wondered what fertilizer the farmer had used. "A magical manure!" he murmured, and blew a kiss to the cows in the nearby field.

But as Henry moved closer, he realized that the glorious peaches were not peaches at all but a pair of pantaloons woven from golden threads. How magnificent—better even than peaches! Henry's eyes gleamed at the sight. He ducked behind a rock, pulled off his overalls, and slipped into the pantaloons.

Henry felt so dashing
that he nearly skipped down
the other side of the hill. When
he reached the bottom, he stopped
short. Did his eyes deceive him? Could
butterflies grow so huge? For it looked as if
giant wings had flopped on the fence post ahead.

As he approached the fence, he saw not a
butterfly but a sumptuously embroidered doublet,
just like those said to be worn in the palace court.
"Pigs in heaven!" exclaimed Henry. And he slipped
his arms into the doublet's sleeves.

Nearby was a pond, its still water as shiny as a mirror. Henry leaned over, peered into the water, and gasped at the exquisite reflection quivering on the surface. *The fish must be dazzled*, he thought. His legs were like those of a bronze statue; his waist seemed smaller and his shoulders broader. What a fine figure he cut.

As Henry stooped to take a drink, a strange fish floated by on top of the water. "The poor fish has been stunned by my handsome figure," Henry whispered. "Oh, dear!"

But it was no fish at all. Henry looked closer. "It's a wig! Oh, glory to geese!" And he pulled it up from the water, shook it out, and plunked it right on his head.

Looking into the water again, Henry arranged the curls just so over his shoulders. "Oh, the animals will love me— the sheep will be entranced, the cow charmed, the goats enchanted. And the chickens will swoon with delight when they see me."

Henry did not know the word *regal*, but that is how he felt—high and mighty, as if he could walk on clouds, as if the mountains would bow and the stars might even clap. But Henry realized that it was getting late, and he had not even passed the palace yet. If he didn't hurry, he would get caught in the crowds watching the emperor's birthday parade.

I *must hurry home*, Henry thought. *Yet . . . I look so wonderful, and I have never before in my life been dressed for court. Perhaps I should just get a glimpse of the festivities.*

So Henry pranced on down the road toward the palace, his curls bouncing, the sunlight glittering on his doublet, his peach pantaloons shimmering, and the ribbons on his high-heeled shoes dancing a jig of their own.

Soon he found himself in the midst of the crowd lining the road.

"Has the parade started?" he asked eagerly.

"Step right up and see for yourself," an old woman replied.

Henry peered through the crowd and blinked in surprise. The emperor was leading the parade, and all the people clapped politely as he strutted by. He flicked his hands as if he were adjusting a doublet. He walked on his toes as if his feet were shod in the highest heels. He lifted his nose into the air as if he were wearing the most stunning finery that anyone had ever seen.

But he was stark naked.

The crowd murmured politely.

"Lovely . . . yes, lovely."

"Such style!"

"Such fashion!"

Henry turned to the old lady in amazement. "Isn't the emperor na—" The old lady put a finger to her lips and blushed.

"Well, I'll be a flea in a donkey's ear!" Henry muttered. "Such foolishness!" And he pushed back through the crowd to continue on his way home.

As Henry neared his farm, he held his head higher and quickened his step. He swept down the path, threw open the gate, and stepped carefully into the barnyard.

They are in awe, Henry thought, for there was not a sound. Not a moo, nor a bleat, nor a cheep. Henry smiled. *They are speechless, bleatless, and cheepless! I am too gorgeous for grunts!*

After taking a moment to enjoy his entrance, Henry began
the chores. But milking the cow was hard; Henry's long curls got
in the way, and he was so busy untangling everything that he
didn't even think to sing the milking song that the cow so dearly
loved. Henry finally wrenched off the wig and tossed it aside.

It was even harder to scatter chicken feed while wearing
his high heels—he had to step so carefully around the cow
patties and the chicks pecking at his feet. And when he
mucked out the stalls, he had to unbutton his
snug doublet.

Then his pantaloons started to billow in the breeze. *I might just lift off!* Henry thought in despair. *Peach pantaloons? More like balloons!* He struggled in the wind, forgetting to say his usual how-do-you-do to his favorite goat, the one whose milk made the creamiest cheese.

The silence seemed to grow heavier while Henry worked. But as he fought his pantaloons, squirmed in his doublet, and stumbled in his shoes, he suddenly realized that the smallest chick was cheeping, and the cheeping was growing louder. And then the chick cackled, fell over, and—was it laughing? Henry, the simple farmer, had never in all his life heard a chicken laugh.

Henry shuddered, then blushed as red as the old lady in the village. He stared down at his knobby old legs in the silk stockings and at the mud on his golden pantaloons. Then he looked around the barnyard at his beloved animals and began to chuckle. The chuckle turned into a giggle, and then a roar, and as Henry ran into his house, his laughter was joined by the joyful bleating, mooing, and cheeping of his animals.

When he returned to the barnyard, he looked like himself again. The cow mooed and swished her tail; the goats and the sheep bleated softly. A hen settled down to lay an egg in the wig Henry had tossed aside.

"That's nice," Henry said.

The hen clucked.

"Thank you, dear," Henry replied, and he thought once again what a blessed man he was.

Library of Congress Cataloging-in-Publication Data
Lasky, Kathryn.
The emperor's old clothes/written by Kathryn Lasky; illustrated by David Catrow.
p.   cm.
Summary: A continuation of "The Emperor's New Clothes" in which a simple farmer finds the
emperor's old clothes on his way home from the market and decides to put them on.
ISBN 0-15-200384-3
[1. Clothing and dress—Fiction. 2. Humorous stories.] I. Catrow, David, ill. II. Title.
PZ7.L3274Em 1999
[E]—dc21   98-5502

First edition
A C E F D B

The illustrations in this book were done in watercolors on bristol board.
The display type was set in Trajan Bold & hand lettered by Judythe Sieck.
The text type was set in Celestia Antigua.
Color separations by Tien Wah Press, Singapore
Printed and bound by Tien Wah Press, Singapore
This book was printed on totally chlorine-free Nymolla Matte Art paper.
Production supervision by Stanley Redfern and Ginger Boyer
Designed by Judythe Sieck